Magnet Magic!

Joseph Stanley

INFOMAX COMMON CORE READERS

Rosen Classroom™

New York

Published in 2014 by The Rosen Publishing Group, Inc.
29 East 21st Street, New York, NY 10010

Book Design: Mickey Harmon

Photo Credits: Cover, p. 17 (magnet) Ivancovlad/Shutterstock.com; cover (background) Charlotte Erpenbeck/Shutterstock.com; p. 5 Rubberball/Mike Kemp/Getty Images; p. 7 TEK IMAGE/Science Photo Library/Getty Images; pp. 9, 13, 15 (paper clip, magnet) iStockphoto/Thinkstock.com; p. 11 Awe Inspiring Images/Shutterstock.com; p. 13 (background) Valentin Agapov/Shutterstock.com; p. 17 (compass) mato/Shutterstock.com; p. 17 (numbers) dubassy/Shutterstock.com; p. 17 (junk yard) worradirek/Shutterstock.com; p. 19 Adolfo Rodriguez Aguilar/Shutterstock.com; p. 21 Gary Ombler/Dorling Kindersley/Getty Images; p. 22 everything possible/Shutterstock.com.

ISBN: 978-1-4777-2341-8
6-pack ISBN: 978-1-4777-2343-2

Manufactured in the United States of America

CPSIA Compliance Information: Batch #CS13RC: For further information contact Rosen Publishing, New York, New York at 1-800-237-9932.

Contents

Science Class

Brynn loves school! Her favorite class is science. Brynn likes science because it teaches her about things in our world. Today in science class, Brynn is learning about magnets! Do you know what magnets are?

It's fun to play with magnets in science class!

What Are Magnets?

A magnet is a piece of **metal** that pulls other metals to it. Some magnets are really big. Others are really small. All magnets are made out of metal. However, not all metals are magnets. Magnets have metals in them such as iron, steel, nickel, or cobalt.

Iron, nickel, and cobalt are some metals found in magnets.

Brynn's teacher gives her a magnet to do an **experiment**. Brynn puts the magnet over a paper clip. It sticks because the paper clip has iron in it. Then, Brynn puts the magnet over a piece of wood. It doesn't stick! The wood doesn't have metal in it.

Magnets can't stick to things like wood or glass, since they don't have magnetic metals in them.

Poles

Brynn's teacher explains that a magnet has two poles. The poles are what pick up iron and steel. Magnets have poles because of the tiny pieces of matter they're made of, called **atoms**. Some atoms go to the magnet's north pole. Other atoms go to the magnet's south pole.

Every magnet has a north pole and a south pole, no matter what shape it is!

N
S

The class does another experiment. Brynn holds two magnets in her hand. She puts one magnet's north pole to the south pole of the other magnet. They **attract**! Then, she flips one magnet over. She can feel the two poles **repel** each other. She can't get them to touch at all!

No matter how hard you try, you can't ever get like poles to stick together!

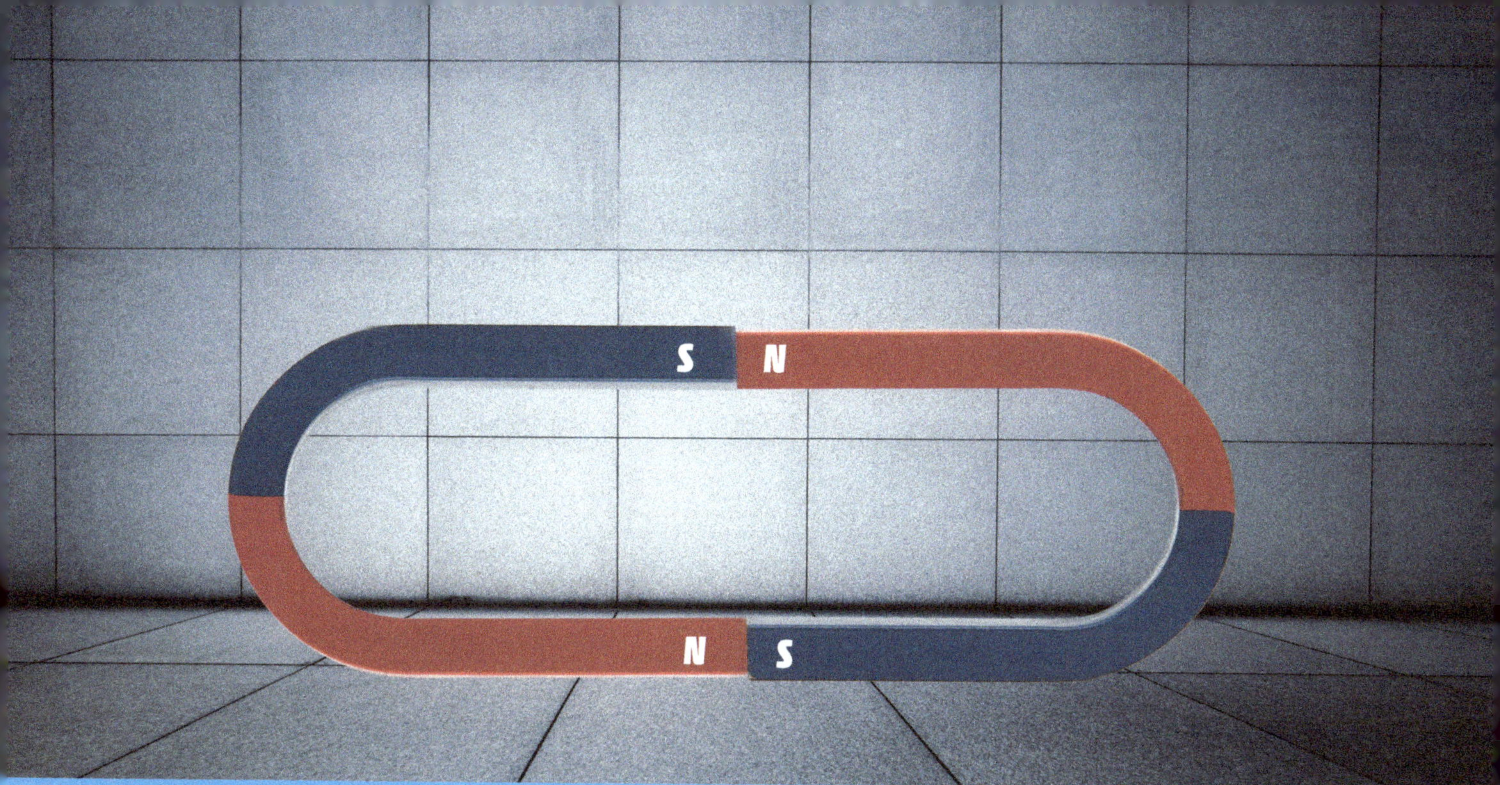
S
N
N
S

N
N
S
S

Brynn feels the magnet get stronger as she moves an object closer. That means the object is within the magnet's **magnetic field**. How strong or weak the magnetic field is depends on how close an object is. The closer Brynn's object gets, the more the magnet attracts it.

A magnet doesn't have to be big to have a strong magnetic field. Some small magnets are really strong!

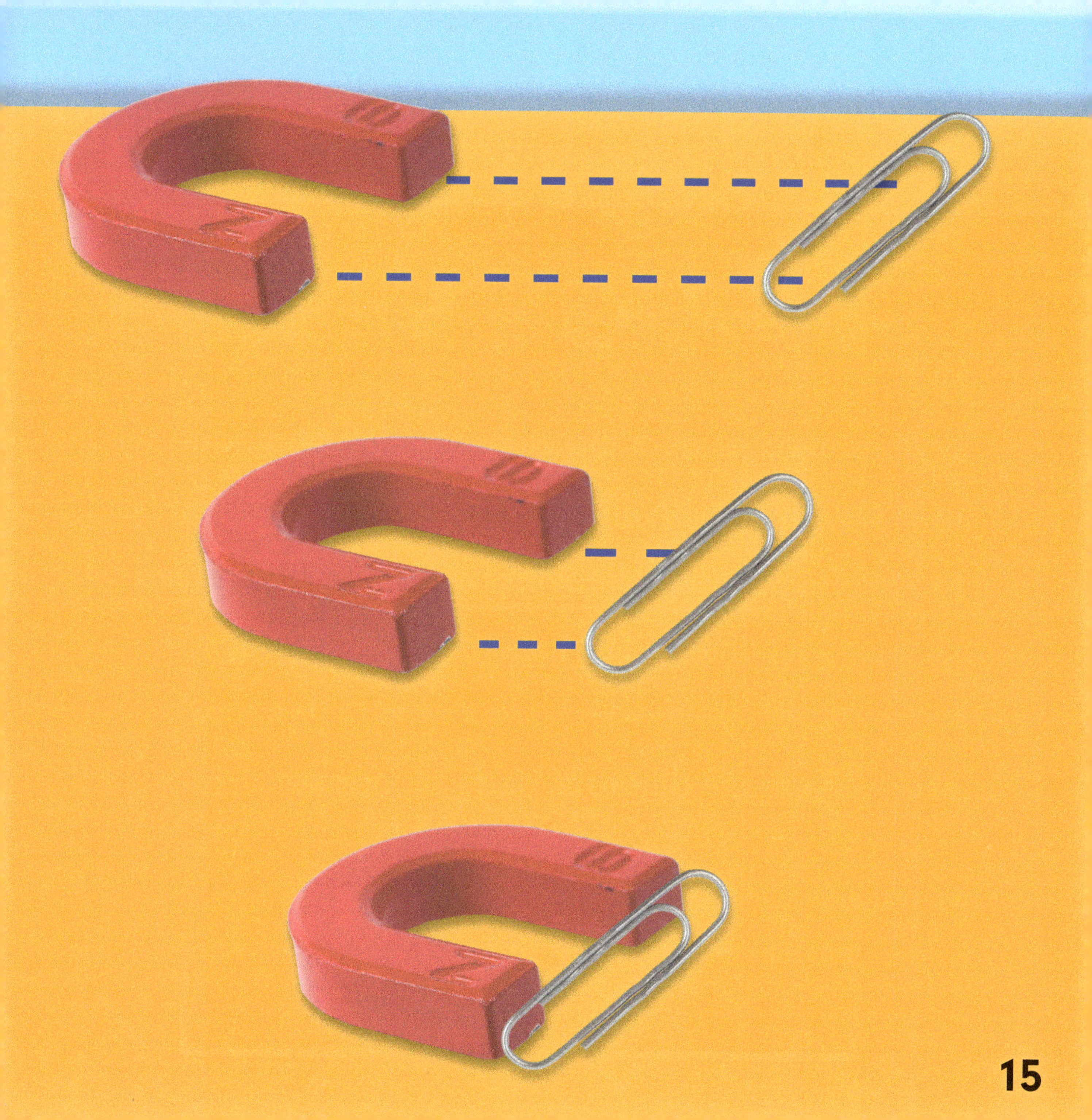

Magnets Are Everywhere!

Brynn's teacher asks the class to think of magnets in everyday life. Brynn says she has magnets on her fridge. They hold pictures of her family. Brynn also knows that some of her toys use magnets. Some tools and computers have magnets in them, too. There are many different kinds of magnets!

What kinds of magnets have you seen in your everyday life?

120
140
160
180
200
220
SE
S
SW
W

S
N

Brynn's teacher says the biggest magnet in the world is Earth's **core**. Earth's core is a magnet because it's made of iron. It's what makes **compasses** work. The magnetic needle in a compass is attracted to Earth's poles. That's why we can always find out where north is.

We can't feel Earth's magnetic field, but it's so strong that it reaches out into space!

20
40
60
80
100
120
140
340
320
300
NE
E
SE
SW
W
NW

Playing with Magnets

The teacher lets the students play with magnets for the rest of class. Brynn and her friends pick up different objects like paper clips, nails, and other things made of metal. They even use compasses! Have you ever played with magnets?

What kinds of things can you pick up with a magnet?

Magnets Are Magic!

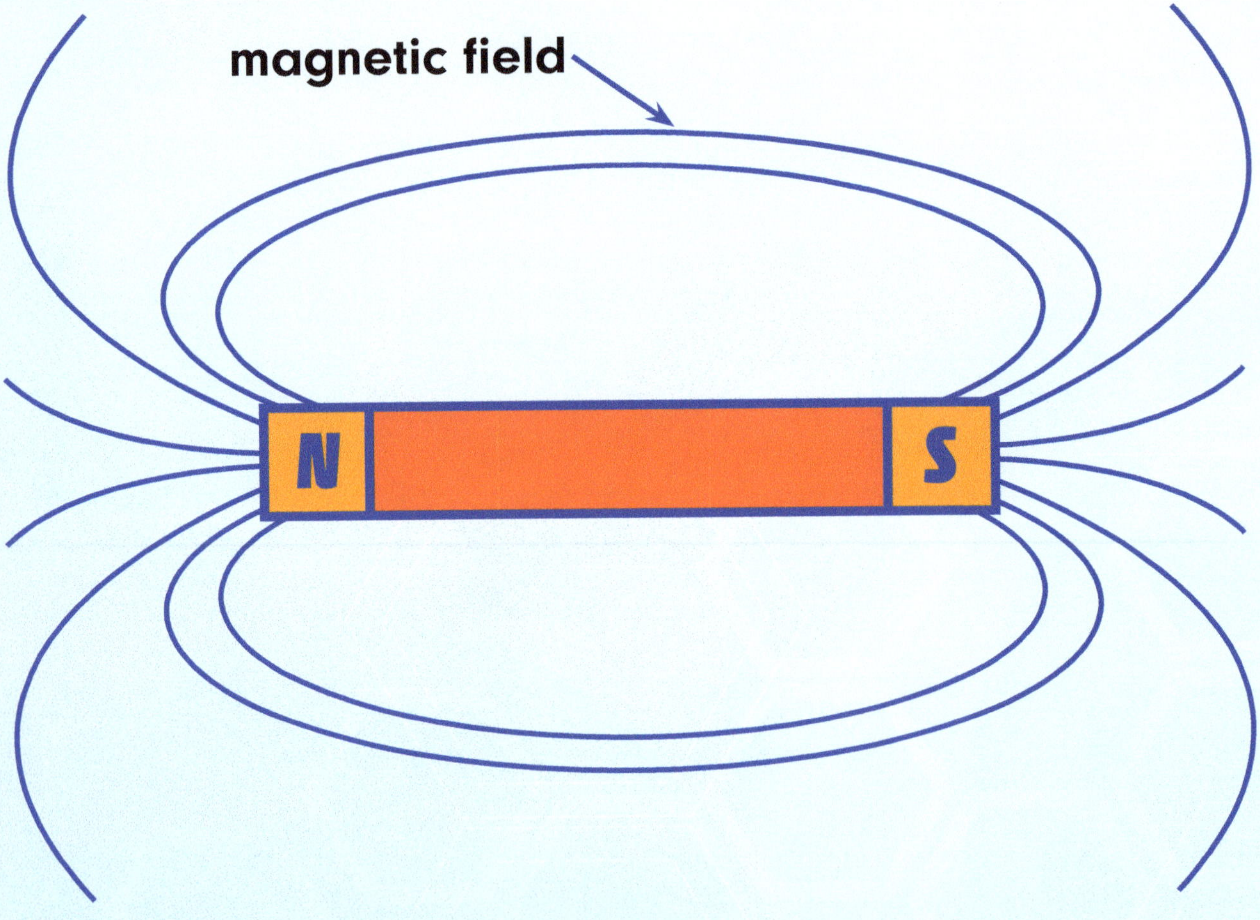

Glossary

atom (A-tuhm) A tiny bit of matter. Everything that exists is made of atoms.

attract (uh-TRAKT) To pull toward.

compass (KUHM-puhs) A tool that shows directions. The needle of a compass always points north.

core (KOHR) The center of something.

experiment (ihk-SPEHR-uh-muhnt) A test to learn about something.

magnetic field (mag-NEH-tihk FEELD) The area around a magnet that attracts objects.

metal (MEH-tuhl) Shiny and hard matter.

repel (rih-PEHL) To push away.

Index